I0625832

THE WET WOMANIZER

A ROMANCE ALONE NOVEL

VISIT US

WWW.GLOFTON.COM
Enroll in our VIP list.
Be the first to be notified on our latest published book.
Downloading for free gifts.

Disclaimer

This is a work of fiction. Names, characters, organizations, spots, occasions and occurrences are either the results of the creator's creative energy or utilized as a part of an invented way. Any similarity to real people, living or dead, or genuine occasions is absolutely adventitious.

ISBN:
eBook: 978-1-946792-12-9
print:978-1-946792-13-6
audio/d :978-1-946792-14-3

Published by Glofton llc

Table Of Content

Wild boy in police uniform
Chapter-1

"Marco, do you know where the tissues are?" Shouted a neighbor Anna, whom I've just screwed in her house. I was proud of what I've done. I screwed her so hard that she limped. "You motherfucker, blood is coming out of my cunt because you cut in there too hard! I was a teenager, a turned on 18 years old teenager. I would catch every chance for a sex that would occur in my life.

I was 18 years old and I was still in a high school. I dressed up and I got out my neighbor's house. It was still summer, beautiful time of year. I would dress more casually.

The reason I was dressing like that was because I felt comfortable that way. I also listened to rap a lot, so that was the reason more. When I walked into school I glanced at the school watch, and I realized I was late.

"Good morning, professor, I'm sorry for being late and for interrupting the lesson."

"And what's the reason this time, you've been too busy writing songs the whole night so you ended up waking up too late?" As soon as the professor said this, whole class went laughing.

"But hey, let's not disrespect this man. I've heard that there is a possibility to earn some money from rap music, 2pac did. I mean, he was the last one who did." The whole class went laughing once again like they were auditory of a sitcom.

This was Professor Larry, an asshole. I didn't disrespect physics, it's a nice science. What was pissing me off, was his behavior. Knowing about the motion of matter and its behavior through space and time was enough for him to think that he was a god. It was clear that he was underestimating me. I didn't like school; I was there just because I had to finish off the education.

The only moments I enjoyed in the school were the ones where we would learn about music, or when we engaged ourselves in physical exercises.

I was about to become a traffic controller. I started this school because others told me there is a bigger potential to earn more money being traffic controller than there is in other professions. Streets of my city were filled with primitivism and negativity.

Hate was almost in the eyes of everyone, and everyone blamed the system only, without being aware of personal mistakes. In my city, there was a common belief that job has to be hated because it's just a job.

Who knows what led to that, but I was wrapped into same belief. I really hated traffic, I hated It so much that I would never engage myself during a practice time in school.

To be honest, there was one thing that I loved about my profession. There is equal interest in being traffic controller, both from girls and guys. In my class, there were fifteen guys and fifteen girls.

There was one super hot girl that was there for the same reason that I was, just to finish off her education, without a particular interest in being traffic-controller.

She was so sexy. She had her hair fastened and her skirt so short that sometimes she would attract everybody's attention.

One day, during practical class she and I were assigned a task to wear police uniforms and get on the road to control traffic.

We were a bit distanced from our city. Standing by the road and controlling cars, we commanded a car to pull over.

When the car stopped, my schoolmate Linda leaned on the front part of the car while she was writing a ticket for a driver. Her butt was visible.

After the car left, I simply couldn't control myself and I asked her if she wants to go with me in the wood that was just by the road, and she agreed.

We were lying on branches that were set on the ground. I was holding my hand in her pants, and she held her hand in my pants. I untied the knot on her hair and I started coming with my cock through it.

"At the end of this, I want to have as much sperm as possible right there where your penis is right now. Be my wind and disperse as much semen as you can on my hair!" She took it with one hand, and then just above that hand with another hand, but still, my cock was so big that she couldn't suck it properly – she couldn't put the whole thing in her mouth.

Standing in that position and taking it in her mouth, she let her one hand on the ground, took a branch and put it down there – where it hurts the most. Even though this girl was young just as I was, she was on fire and ready for any kind of challenge.

Afterward, I grabbed my penis and took it between her breast. Her breast was like watermelons.

They were round, big, and wet. While I was going up between her breast, she was caressing it. I put my finger inside her, fingered her as hard as I could. She was releasing sounds of pleasure. Some kind of liquid started coming out of her pussy. I put it down and I made my penis wet as I entered her vagina.

I was screwing her for forty-five minutes, she almost passed out but she still wanted more. We already had all the branches beneath us broken, so everything beneath us was just scratching our bodies, but we didn't stop. I ejaculated on her hair as she was smiling just as she wanted to say that we need to do that again.

"Look at him, he is staring into river already for two minutes. Is he paralyzed?"

Two girls commented on my behavior while I was sitting and waiting for my bus. I stared in that river because I was too tired.

Every girl that I was in touch with wanted me to satisfy her needs. After a hard night, a girl that I spent the night with would brag about how she had an incredible night.

I knew that these intentionally loud comments on me were with the intention to get them screwed.

I felt bad that I couldn't give it to these girls as they were playing with their hair while looking at my pants. I knew that I was better than their boyfriends, even though I didn't have as big muscles as their boyfriends had. I had a little bit skinnier body, but it made me fast and ready to provide girls with a night full of a beautiful pain!

Walking the narrow hall that led to the GYM where I used to work out made me see a guy and a girl making it out, they were kissing each other. She was sitting in his lap and he was sitting on the edge of a thick fence.

"Wear something heavy, it's windy outside. The wind could make you fly." Said the guy.

I just looked at him and continued walking.

I started thinking: "If this guy knew what I do to his girlfriend every week, he wouldn't have teased me. He would respect my physics but he would still want to beat the crap out of me for screwing his girlfriend."

He doesn't stop until it's wet
Chapter-2

Living life like this I started reading about GYM. I started finding out solutions for my body problems. I didn't want to be skinny anymore.

I was sure that I was going to become what I wanted the most – A model. I wanted to become a famous model. I didn't dare to tell these things to anyone, I knew that nobody would understand this.

I worked on my look and I realized that I had to work on my mass in order to reach my goal. I started going to GYM. When I entered the GYM for the first time, I didn't know how to get to the room where people do exercises.

I was walking through a hall and everything was dark. All the sudden, I started seeing some lights on the walls.

There were some posters. A first thing that I took a look at, was a poster with a picture of Nelson Mandela with the following description: "It always seems impossible until it's done. – Nelson Mandela."

Walking through the hall led me to another poster:

"I've missed more than 9000 shots in my career. I've lost almost 300 games. 26 times, I've been trusted to take the game-winning shot and missed. I've failed over and over and over again in my life. And that is why I succeed. - Michael Jordan."

As I was approaching the training room I've seen something that motivated me more than anything before.

"I don't mind people hating me because it pushes me. – Cristiano Ronaldo". Along with this inscription, a picture of the confident face of Cristiano was filling the big poster on the wall.

I approached the door of the exercise room. I was holding the doorknob while hundreds of thoughts came to my mind in only a few seconds. I felt incredible fear but I didn't hesitate much to get into the exercise room.

I heard some unknown voices as a sound of weight being put on the floor made me realize that I was at the right place. Coach told me that first exercise that I should take is cardiovascular exercise. I started running on a machine with a track fixed to it. There was another machine standing just by me, and a girl running on it.

"The speed." She said.

"Speed?"

"You should reduce the speed of the track. You're running too fast for a beginner."

"Let me do it for you." She stopped running and approached my machine. She was standing in a front of me while explaining to me how to handle the machine. I didn't hear a word.

I was staring at her well-shaped body which made me wonder how much it took her to look like that.

"How long do you train?" I asked while we were running together.

"Two years."

"Wow, you accomplished a lot in only two years."

"Don't you try to seduce me." She smiled. I think that having that smile in the GYM made every second of pain, moan and sigh less painful. I was going from one machine to another, getting familiar with what I should do. The GYM was definitely the most positive place that I've been at, along with the boxing hall that I was visiting every day.

Away from insults, bad habits and everything negative, I stepped on the path of success. Lifting weights made me feel a lot of pain. There was something different in this pain, I enjoyed it.

I differentiate two kinds of people: The ones that temporarily work for eternal joy, and the ones that perpetually work for eternal joy. An example of people that temporarily work for eternal joy would be people like me.

I go to GYM to develop my muscles and to look good. I will have to do that maybe for three years to get the best of my body. After that, I will not have to work anymore, I will have a perfect body attracting women and bringing respect into my life. On the other side, the guy that perpetually works for eternal joy is someone who derives joy from let's say, eating chips and drinking alcohol every day.

Not only that he will have to do that every time he wants to feel the joy, but it will lead him to sickness and bad physical condition overall.

Setting up priorities in my head and thinking what to start with in order to get where I want to be was interrupted by the coach's voice.

"Do you need any help?"

"Thanks, but I'm doing well for now."

"Nice to hear man, just keep pushing."

I picked up my towel and headed towards the exit of the exercise room. I stopped at the hall and covered my face with the towel, wiping the sweat.

All of the sudden, someone removed the towel from my head.

"How old are are you? You pretty boy." Asked the girl that gave me the guide on how to handle the machine for running.

"I'm 18."

"Well, you see, I've shown you how to handle some machines, and I don't want you to pay me for that service." She said this while looking at my belly touching it with her hands."

"No no, I'm sorry. I shouldn't have forgotten. I will pay you for the guide."

"You will make it up in the bathroom. I presume that you never had a sex. Am I right?" The lust in her eyes played with her tongue as she was saying the dirtiest, and to my ears, the most beautiful things to hear.

Even thought that I had a plenty of sex every week, thinking that virgins maybe turn her on, I lied that it was my first time."

"I'm feeling a little bit uncomfortable at this moment. Where do we do that?" She took my hand and led me to the girl's bathroom. We went to the shower. Before we even got naked, I was kissing her and touching the intimate parts of her beautiful body in a clumsy manner.

"Oh my good, your body is so perfect. Did you bring condoms?"

"I have them all time in my bag, you never know when you're going to end up under the shower, do you?" She said while giving me a box of condoms.

I got naked first. I didn't have a nice body, but at least my face was pretty. I guess that was the reason she seduced me. I stripped her bra while she was unfastening a knot that was holding her hair. I was kissing her breast while she was sighing and moving her long and beautiful hair behind her ears.

She put her head in a tilt position as she was embracing my body with her tattooed hands. I was moving to her belly as her long hair was touching my back. I put her GYM suit down leaving her only with panties.

I ripped the thinnest part of her panties that covered the deepest secret of her intimacy. I was exploring everything that mattered to me in those moments, giving her a pleasant punishment for underestimating the power of a young man.

Then I let her feel my body. She started touching my abs and experimenting with the inmost part of my body. Drops of the water from the shower were killing drops of the sweat that we incurred.

She incurred it by running and shaping the parts of her body and making them thrilling for the pleasure that comes, and I incurred it by lifting the weights.

She stood with her breast against the wall while I put a condom entering the gates of desired pleasure.

I did it hard and clumsy, so she screamed the same moment. She bit her lip as she turned her head to me smiling.

"That's the way men should treat women. Push harder!"

It lasted one hour. After that everything was wet, including her GYM clothes. There were the moments when she wanted to stop because it was not easy for her to have an orgasm, but I didn't let her give up. The persistence made me give her the best orgasm she ever had.

At the end, she was lying in my hands as I kissed her hair that had an aroma of peach, thanks to the shampoo she used.

"Tell me about your goal."

"What goal?"

She looked deeply into my eyes as she kissed me and put an alight cigarette in my mouth.

"Nobody comes here just like that. You must have a goal that you want to accomplish by exercising. I am going here to be attractive to men. What's that that you're looking forward to?" She asked with a beautiful smile on her face.

"I want to... Actually, it doesn't matter, I don't tell that to anyone."

"Why?"

"Because I feel like everyone will tease me. They will think it's impossible."

"Nothing is impossible." With these words, she encouraged me to reveal my dream to her.

"Well, you see, I want to become a model. That's why I decided to come here and get some mass. I want to have a handsome body." I said

"I'm not going to preach you about the possibility of it, I'll just show you what I looked like, and you are certainly the best judge to evaluate the progress that I made because you've seen and felt my body completely."

She found some pictures on her phone and showed them to me. When she just started, she looked worse than I look now.

If someone told me that the girl from the GYM will provide me with so much of pleasure and motivation, I wouldn't have believed him.

Since I was trying to gain weight and get a muscular body, I was reading a lot about it. Going to the GYM every day improved not only my physical look, it improved my self-esteem as well.

His intelligence turned me on
Chapter-3

We were at a class of psychology when our professor asked if there is someone that would define hatred.

"So there is John raising his hand. All right John, tell us a little bit about this emotion."

"Hatred is a negative emotion that one feels when there is a difference around him, a difference that he doesn't like."

"Interesting answer John. Is there anyone else who would like to say something about hatred?"

"Hatred is a division once emerged, accepted as right and desirable, perceived without its negative effects, even though everyone was aware of them. A drug is hatred to a body; laziness is hatred to the spirit of the body. A bullet is a hatred to tissue, and ground is hatred to the throne.

Now let's get a little bit deeper into social interactions, if primitivism is undesired and if fairness matters, why do we spit on each other? Fight emerges between good and bad, and bad was perceiving itself as good, and such perception was bad, which is why it led to a fight.

"Please give this man applause." Said professor while taping with his palms. The only person that applauded with a professor was Marie.

"You're so, you're..." Stammered fat Fred.

Everyone was looking at me with astonishment in their eyes.

What really mattered to me in that situation was applause from the most beautiful girl from in class, Marie. Marie was a combination of beauty and intelligence.

I've never seen so much of amazing characteristics in one person. Not only was she beautiful and intelligent, but also a model of morality.

Nevertheless, she was never showing appreciation for something that she doesn't like. Therefore, her behavior made me feel that she likes me.

We used to have a few classes of "professional practice" in a raw. Those were depressive days for me because I really hated the lessons. We had 30 minutes of pause between classes of practice. During that time I used to visit a coffee shop where you could order a coffee and use a computer for free. I was listening to songs in which I would find myself, most of the time I was listening to rap music. I was searching for inspiration to write songs.

A trash can in the coffee shop was full of papers, every day. During the day I would write songs, and during the night I would do exercises in the GYM.

One sunny morning before the school time, I went to a restaurant to eat. I was eating a pie when a man in a blue suit approached me and asked if he can sit to eat with me, and I agreed.

Since I had a problem with low self-esteem, I was shy and it was hard for me to look in somebody's eyes. Therefore, in this situation, I was just eating and looking around. I felt really uncomfortable. This man was analyzing me; he was looking straight into my eyes while he was eating his pie.

"Are you at the university?"

"No, I'm still in a high school."

"Are you planning to continue your education?"

"I'm not sure, there are only a few classes that I like."

"You seem very clever." Said he.

"How do you know that I'm clever when we have just met for the first time?"

"One can recognize it in the eyes."

"Thank you."

"Is there a chance for you to continue your education?"

"Yes, well, If I get better at school I might be able to continue with my education."

"I think that would be an option." Not a long time after he said this, he took his plate, handed it to the worker of the restaurant, and he left.

It was the first time that something like this happened to me. People in my city are most of the time reserved, and I could never imagine something like this happening to me. Nevertheless, I was glad that this happened.

This man encouraged me, I was studying hard every day. It really was a struggle. I hated most of the studying time, but I knew that once I get to the university that I like, a majority of what I will study, will be something that I love.

I decided to study sports and physical education. Weeks were coming by and I was getting better and better. I was growing bigger and I was getting smarter.

Some people started to respect me, but also, an amount of the people that hated me was increased. People were jealous and they couldn't stand me.

He makes my world spinning
Chapter-4

Geography, all those countries, rivers, and planets didn't really matter to our super sexy teacher. Ms. Laura used to spread her legs very often. She would take a stick and bite it. A sexual desire was screaming out of her. She had a husband but she was getting laid at every place she could. This week, I was the victim.

I wanted to sacrifice my balls in order to provide this lady with a pleasure. When class was finished, I was the last one left in a classroom packing up my things.

She approached me and put the peak of her stick on my penis. She stripped off everything she had on the upper part of her body. I was playing with my tongue; I was treating her boobs like a kid would treat candies.

"Teacher, you're superior. Those boobs are constantly distracting my attention during the class, and now, I finally have them in my hands."

"Enough of talk, now come into my hands."

She stripped me off completely. I was lying on a table as she was making my penis wet, I didn't ejaculate yet, but her mouth was making it wet.

After that, I was kissing her butt. Simply, there wasn't a part of her body that I didn't touch. I grabbed her beautiful panties that were hot because of the temperature of her vagina.

I stripped them off and I started punishing her with a stick! I was sticking it in every little beautiful hole that was on her body. She was screaming out.

"You're better than my husband, just keep going on with it!"

I put her in a position where she was touching the wall, with her back against my biggest intimate part. I was giving it so hard to her that her boobs were hitting the wall constantly and they became white.

"Oh, you're trying to destroy my vagina?"

"All right, I'll recover you."

I put her on the table as I put my tongue inside her vagina. I was giving her pleasure with my tongue until she reached orgasm. The whole table was wet; she was so screwed that her legs were shaking. But she wanted more. Two minutes afterward, the director of the school entered the classroom.

Since he already had a sex with her, he wasn't wondering what happens. He put his pants off and simply started work. He had a penis of a huge size. He was going so hard on her that table almost broke apart. His penis was so big that she couldn't stand taking it in her vagina, so he approached her from her back, going on her ass.

At the same time, I was putting my penis in her vagina. Director and I destroyed her. After each of us had an orgasm, director and I kept lying with her on the floor, playing with her boobs, as she was recovering from hard sex.

Rain outlines his big muscles
Chapter-5

Even though I've slept with many girls, it was just a sex. I didn't love them. This time, I felt something more toward one girl.

After an exhausting day in the school, holding a cheeseburger in my hand   I was exiting a fast food. It was rainy outside.

I saw Marie walking by the wall of the fast food. In order to get protected, she was walking under eaves of the building.

"Why don't you carry an umbrella? You will get wet." I asked her with a smile on my face, trying to be as polite as possible.

"I forgot it at home."

"Do you want to go for a walk with me? We are quite similar, but we don't hang out at all. Don't you think that it should change?"

I think that this was the most confident sentence that I ever said in my life. I amazed myself by saying it.

"Why not? Let's go for a walk" Said she.

"Let me first buy you something to eat while we're still here by the fast food."

"No, I'm not hungry." She said.

"If you don't feel hungry, how do you feel then?"

"A bit tired and stressed out." She said.

She was very positive; she would smile all the time although her life wasn't perfect. Her father was dead and she had medical problems.

"Why are you stressed out?"

"I don't know, it's just that I study all the time. I don't have time to hang around."

"Can I ask you something?"

"Anything you want, Marco."

"How come you're so good?"

"I'm not good to everyone. I'm good to you because you're a good person."

"Do you ever think of leaving this city?"

"Sometimes I visualize that I am at a better place. Why do you ask? Don't you like it here?" She asked.

"I don't know. Don't you think that people are bad here?"

"Everybody is aware of it, everybody except them. Since the majority of people are bad, only a few persons are left to realize the truth."

"Would you be my girlfriend?"

I don't know how come this came out of me but the same moment I said it, I regretted. I was thinking that it wasn't time for such question since that is the first time we had a private conversation.

"Yeah, why not?" I was surprised by her answer.

She hug me immediately as she whispered magic words to my ears:

"Do you know how much I wanted this? Earlier, I liked your character only, you're such a visionary. A few months ago, just looking at you made me feel turned on. I don't know what are you doing, but last few months you look super sexy." The same moment she said that I threw my umbrella away and I kissed her.

As the sky was raining and thunder stroke made us look at a glowing line on the dark sky, I kissed her. The wind was throwing her hair as a good beat awakes adrenaline in the body of a human being letting its legs defy lights of a dance floor.

I stripped off my jacket and I put it on her body. I took her hand as we were running toward an unknown building to hide from the rain.

Her head was in my lap. Two bodies on 37 degrees of temperature lying in a wooden and decayed house that is exposed to millions of rain drops. Only a few chosen drops were dripping down the gutter, and listening to it didn't make me a chosen one, but still, it made me feel special.

I put my hand on her belly and I started caressing her. I was kissing her neck as she was twisting. She was wearing slim tight pants that were wet because of the rain. That made her ass so outlined. I embraced her back and I put hands down to her butt. I was squeezing it so hard that drops of the rain were coming out of her pants.

I couldn't help myself so I started putting it inside immediately. We didn't need to go around that much because we were already completely wet. She was holding her hands on my shoulders as I held her body in my hands making sure that she's feeling it inside.

She shed a few tears as I ejaculated on her boobs. She said that she regrets that she didn't do this with me even before.

"Why do you let them tease you?"

"I don't know, I'm just not used to conflicts."

"You have to stand four yourself. Why don't you arrange a rap battle?"

I looked into her eyes curiously.

"Do you really think that I can make it?"

"You're the most talented rapper and writer that I know."

"How did you come up with that idea?" I asked Marie.

"You weren't at the music class today, were you?"

"No, I wasn't there."

"Well, you see, everyone was assigned a task to write a song and perform the song, next class. You can choose a rap song. That way you will show everyone that you're not afraid to participate a rap battle.

You will also show them that you possess skills. That on the music class is not going to be a battle, only a performance because the teacher wants to evaluate our singing skills."

"Can't believe. I missed the best class. Let's get out of here. I don't have time to waste. I must go and write something good."

We got out, we picked the bus and split. She went back to her house; I went to the coffee shop to write.

I was thinking a lot about Marie. Pictures of the life were coming through my head. I realized how many things were out there that didn't really matter. I was thinking about beautiful moments when I was kissing Marie. I was thinking how life is empty. So many moments pass, and we don't even feel them. It's sad. It's like empty trains riding and empty planes flying. All of the things that our society consider as a must, such as days of flirting and days of pretending made no sense in my head. I asked Marie simply if she wants to be my girlfriend, and she agreed.

I think that every person in space and time knows what he/she wants. I think that if she didn't like me just a few moments before I asked her if she wants to be my girlfriend, she wouldn't like me after a few days of flirting either.

One day, while I was sitting in front of the computer in the coffee shop and writing songs, someone approached me and put a hand on my eyes.

"Who's that? Maybe someone trying to steal my ideas?" I said.

"Maybe someone trying to steal your heart?" I recognized the voice, that was Marie.

Come on, sit next to me. I said after I kissed her.

I was showing her the things that I wrote.

"That song is good, but while performing it in front of the classmates, you need to point at specific people, at the ones that have been organizing rap battle for years. You need to provoke best rappers in the class" - Said Marie

"Paul and Steve definitely. Since I met them for the first time, two things were obvious about them: They are most famous organizers of the rap battles, and they are the biggest assholes that I ever met."

"That's true, but don't forget Eric. Even though he isn't that much into rap, saying something about him will make him pissed off, and he will definitely persuade Paul and Steve to organize a battle. He also knows everybody in the school, he will invite everyone to watch the battle hoping that you get dissed,"

After a few moments of silence, she embraced my head and whispered:

"I'm going to make sure that you win." She added.

We spent next two hours sitting in the coffee shop and putting aside rhymes that didn't fit.

Marie was a girl with style. She would always combine her clothes well. I was wearing loose clothes all the time, the clothes that are typical for rappers.

She had never expressed any opinion about my way of dressing. Anyway, just a day before the class where I was supposed to provoke a rap battle I wanted to buy some clothes.

I asked Marie if she wants to go with me, and she agreed. Despite not having a big mass on my body, I was a tall guy.

Being tall led to having many problems with choosing best clothes.

Marie thought that black loose pants would fit good with a hoodie that was a combination of black and white color. I bought white shoes as well, and I was ready for stepping in front of my classmates and showing my classy style.

A genius with big penis
Chapter-6

Yesterday is gone. Rhymes, along with my boosted confidence were the part of the new day, the day I was up to provoke a battle.

That day I was completely on fire, full of inspiration and willing to stand for myself.

The first class was physics, I missed it intentionally. I knew that presence of professor of physics could only have a negative effect on me during such important day.

Classes were passing and those that I participated, I was only physically present in the classrooms. My spirit was on the stage along with my thoughts.

"It's your last high school grade. Soon we will split up and all the negative and positive memories will start fading as the future brings new challenges and new experiences. There's something that I want to do before you leave this school with your diplomas. I want to see your singing abilities. All of you were assigned a task to write a song that you will perform today." As professor Christine walked through the classroom saying all of this, she noticed me.

"Marco Casanova, you were absent at the last class. Are you notified by any of your classmates about today's music performance?"

"Yes Ms. Christine, I've been notified by Marie." As I was saying this, everybody was looking at me with serious expressions on their faces. Just like they wanted to say: "We can finally see about your skills. You talked about rap all the time but you never sang anything."

That is true, I never dared to step out and sing something, I was just too shy with low self-esteem. During the last few months, I transformed myself into someone bigger, not just someone with a bigger body, but also someone with guts.

The class was passing and many songs were played on our little stage in the classroom. Most of the time, girls would sing songs of a pop genre. The majority of guys performed rap songs, some of them were even up on the stage with rock songs. I was the last one to step on the stage.

"Everybody pay attention, it's not over yet, there is one song left. I want to welcome to the stage Marco Casanova, the last one informed about this event and the last one stepping on the stage.

I took a microphone in my right hand.
For the first few seconds, I was just holding
that microphone without saying a thing.
Emotions just escalated and I started singing:

I stand for what I believe,

Paul, Eric, and Steve,

Dropping heavy rhymes on you,

Is what I tend to achieve,

If what you do is good,

Then I'm the biggest thieve.

I've been running for too long,

I've been dropping the pen,

Couldn't be strong,

But I came up with a song,

I rap so fast that you think

You're watching a ping pong.

You're waving your hands,

Getting no support,

And you ask what's wrong,

No answer but one thing is sure,

As long as I'm here

Your misery I will prolong.

You think you have talent?

What? Stop tripping.

Your talent is absent

You guys are silent,

Cause when I drop the rhyme,

My clock works faster

Your heads are rusted,

Now I'm done,

I mean, done is the master.

Everyone was looking at Paul and Steve, some of them observed Eric too.

"Steve, is this a sign that there is someone better than you?"

"Hey Eric, how can you stand this? Your reputation is coming down."

"You guys just got dissed."

"Paul, this guy is a tough competition, don't you think so?"

These were the voices from my classmates. My reputation grew up a little bit.

"Well, this was amazing. I mean, it's not that I like these dissing lines, but this was very original. How did you come up with this?" Asked professor Christine.

"I wanted to show these people that when it comes to words, they are only good with insults."

As soon as I said this, the whole class started shouting:

"We want a rap battle, we want a rap battle, we want a rap battle!"

Everyone was shouting this, except Steve, Paul, and Eric.

Finally, Steve stood up, looked over and with a confident smile said:

"All right, you want to see me dissing this guy? You really want it?"

Everyone shouted: "Yes we want, beat his ass." Everyone, except Marie.

Even though people were cheering after I finished the song, they still liked Steve more. Being considered as the best rapper in the class for past few years, made him have all of that respect.

I was still on the stage when Marie came up to me and hugged me. This is the first time that people saw us together.

"Oh look, seems like he has support, he isn't alone." This one and similar sentences resounded the class.

"All right people: Friday, 7 p.m. at the stadium behind the school, a rap battle between me and Steve. Everyone is welcome." I said this in front of the whole class loudly so everyone could hear it.

The class ended, and as days passed, the tension was still present between me and Steve, each day growing bigger and bigger.

He makes it nasty down there
Chapter-7

I went to the coffee shop again. The first day of writing was really hard. I couldn't write anything; I was under some kind of pressure. This time I really had to engage myself, it was an important day, high school was about to end, and I wanted to win that battle. She was with me all the time. Marie was coming with me in the coffee shop.

She would just look at me and smile while I was writing with my face being pretty serious. Days were coming by and I was falling in love with her. Those days I felt more like writing some romantic songs, but that wasn't what I needed for the battle.

She was of a huge help, having her as a support made me feel great. Well, I would single out some moments when she was distracting me. Seeing me so serious and dedicated to writing was turning her on.

When I was in a middle of my writing she would grab my t-shirt and she would pull me toward her body.

In those moments, her kisses would eliminate all the hate I felt for the guys in my class that used to tease me all the years in the high school. She was just spontaneous.

She would kiss me in front of the crowd without caring how many people are looking at us. She had a completely different mindset from the rest of the people living in my city.

It was Thursday, the day before the rap battle. The class was very loud; everyone was talking about the upcoming event. Everybody was thrilled, everybody but Marie. She was sad the whole day. Seeing her like that, made me wonder what's going on. As usually, after the school time was over, I went to GYM.

Since I had a girlfriend, I didn't let any other woman get too close to me. The girl that I slept with when I had my first training in the GYM was trying to get close to me.

She was smiling every time I was in the GYM, she would bite her lip and play with her hair while looking at me, but I would just refuse to flirt.

That day, I was working on my chest. I was sitting on a bench, lifting heavy weights. When I was done, someone embraced my belly and touched my body. It was her, the girl that didn't even tell me her name although we were so close the first day in the GYM.

"Is there something wrong with me? You don't like me anymore?"

"No, it's not that I don't like you. It's just.."

"It's just what?"

"I have a girlfriend."

"Come on, she doesn't have to know."

"No way. I want to be loyal to her."

"What about the night under the shower? You didn't like it?"

"No, I liked it, but things are different now."

While we had this conversation, all of the sudden, Marie showed up the GYM. She just looked at me, shed a tear, and left without saying a word.

"Wait! Marie, wait!"

She didn't stop. I wanted to explain her things but she just ignored me.

The day of the rap battle was there. Friday, last day of the school, time to show my guts. It was a time for revenge. I woke up full of self-esteem.

I was standing in front of a mirror practicing for the rap battle. I was looking straight in my eyes while pronouncing every word of my final rap song.

"Marco, leave the bathroom! You must go to school." My mom said. These words interrupted me, but right on time, because I've had enough of practice. It was time for me to go out.

"I believe in you." I've repeated this sentence three times, and I walked out of the bathroom.

The whole class went mad about the event. There wasn't a single person that wasn't talking about it. This time I was left with no support. Once again, all alone, but this time walking toward the throne.

The brave guy with charisma
Chapter-8

Last seconds of our last class passed. High school was over. It wasn't over for me, that night was more important than anything. As soon as I heard school bell I walked out of the school. It was a bell that denoted the end of the match. Nevertheless, a bell in my head denoted that this match has no winner, and the last round is yet to come.

With a hoodie cap on my head, dressed like a warrior fighting with his words I started walking toward the stadium.

I had that moment, once again unfairly left aside I stepped my leg on the stadium and walked through the middle of the crowd. There were so many people. My city had many high schools and I had a feeling that every teenager from my city came right there to watch this battle. Everyone was familiar with my story.

Everyone knew what I've been through and that I'm here for a revenge. As I was walking through the crowd I've encountered different reactions from different people. Some of them were screaming out: Marco, this is your night, show them what you can! Almost everyone was touching me, wanting to shake hands with me.

A host was standing on a stage, along with Steve.

Walter, the guy that made a couple of albums was the host of this battle. He was an announcer, and judge of the battle as well.

"Put your hands in the air for the second competitor, Marco Casanova!"

I went on stage, grabbed a microphone and said:

"It's a little bit hard to talk right now as talking is needless when we have what?" I turned microphone toward the public.

"Rap battle" Crowd was repeating this line until Walter took over the microphone.

"The first one who is going to perform his song tonight is Steve Jones!"

"Steve, the stage is yours." The judge said as he handed him the microphone.

Steve:

Hey Pal, take a necklace

And try to shine,

Your style is glowing as dark,

And your success goes no further,

Than to a fault line.

The way you walk is so funny,

That you look like you

Stepped on a mine,

You're so happy,

that your face

looks like a brine,

You beg me to wipe my ass,

but I decline.

You act like you have a pride,

But the car you drive

Makes you be classified as someone

with no ride.

You think that you can lift

Bigger weight,

Fuck it homie,

now you're the one

Full of hate.

Your history is poor

Your future is without rate,

Come on mate,

drop the microphone,

Before it gets too late.

We're bigger than you,

You have the doors

While we have the gate,

You knew that good was evil,

But you didn't want to cooperate.

The whole crowd cheered. The atmosphere became really noisy.

"That was Steve Jones. Now, the second competitor will take the microphone and light up the atmosphere, Marco Casanova!

Marco, grab this microphone and shine!"

Before I said anything, the microphone was producing a creaking sound. After a few moments, it was working once again properly.

"I just want to say something, before I start singing."

"Come on, we don't want to wait." Someone from the crew shouted.

"Marie, if you're out there, I just want to say that I love you."

I had taken my hoodie cap off and I started singing:

The first day it was hard

For me to write,

But this line was right:

Seeing me with a microphone,

Makes you uptight.

Loading up your gun,

Showing up only at night,

Makes me diss you pussy,

Your ugly face was the reason

Your dick never saw the light.

You're afraid and you scream out:

Please, Marc, get out of my sight

If you stay a few more seconds

By that microphone,

My positive future

May never catch the flight.

DJ turn that shit

And please don't promote him,

I'm taking it to the throne,

As I send pictures to this sinker

'Cause that might comfort him.

He's moving forth and back

Like worms are in his ass,

Look at what skills he possess,

He used to diss me for my look,

But take a look at his mass.

He is bold as fuck,

Girls are running away from him,

But he won't confess.

Your existence is a failure,

Your birth was unplanned highway,

Looking at a picture of my dick,

Is for your happy start of a new day.

Now this rhyme is a kick in your head,

Wipe your tears and go back to your bed.

Incredible noise resounded from the stadium. People went so loud that people from outside the stadium thought there is some riot going on.

People were cheering and I enjoyed it.

"Wait, wait, wait! I must declare the winner." Said Walter, but nobody heard what he was saying because it was too loud there.

After two minutes, auditory finally lowered the noise.

"Now, I know that this is a big moment for both of you, and I just want you to know that no matter who wins, you were both incredible tonight," Said Walter.

Now, I see that auditory is a little bit impatient, so I will go on with the declaration" He added after a few moments of silence.

"And the winner of this rap battle is..."

Silence covered the stadium for a few seconds.

"The winner of this rap battle is Marco Casanova."

People were shouting my name.

"Marco, Marco, Marco!" I've never felt bigger. That day will stay forever in my memory. The day when I showed that few of my lines are worth more than any of their insults.

My happiness didn't last long because when I woke up, I heard something that I will never forget.

I was riding a bike when a guy from the school stopped me.

"Hi, Marco."

"Hi, Kevin, what's up?"

"Nothing special man. I want to congratulate you! You were great last night.

"Thanks, man, you were there too?"

"Yes, Of Course, I was there. I'm sorry for your girlfriend. It's horrible that such things are happening to good people like she is."

"Wait, what happened to Marie?"

"How come you don't know? Everyone is talking about her disease."

"Disease? What disease?"

"She has leukemia. Chances are low that she will survive."

The same moment he said this, I sat myself down on the sidewalk. I was staring at the floor. This time I wasn't staring because I was too tired by having too much of sex. I stared at the floor because I was shocked by the fear of losing her.

I was shocked by the fear of losing someone that mattered so much, that I started to practice sex in a moderate manner, aiming my sexual desire only at one person, at my girlfriend Marie.

The same day I went to her house, but she didn't want to talk with me. I was sitting there for 3 hours but she ignored me completely.

After that, suffering was the only thing that was left to me.

Womanizer alone with six girls
Chapter-9

I was studying sports and physical education. Three years passed since I started my studies. 21 years old, a decent man.

I had all of those muscles, I had a potential.

High school memories were. Ambitious as always. My main focus was GYM. I was a pretty serious man. I didn't have a girlfriend, but I had so many girls considering me as their friend, and we were friends beneath the blanket. I would hang out with them all the time.

One day while I was lifting weights, I heard a speech of an unknown voice: "Look at those muscles. Look at that mass. So, you're that guy who wants to become a model?"

I looked at him at the moment and I continued lifting weights.

"Do you really think that it's wise to ignore someone who has come to give you a chance?"

"What chance?"

"Whatever you want. There has to be a goal. I can see passion in you."

I stopped lifting the weights.

"My name is Marco, Marco Casanova."

"I know who you are. I'm Victor, I've been a professional advisor in the industry of fashion for fifteen years. I've helped many people to become models. I can train you as well. Of Course, if you want."

"Leave me your number, I will call you tomorrow to tell you what I've decided. " I said.

"All right. Don't forget to contact me."

After the training, I decided to have some fun. I called all of my female friends and arranged orgy at my apartment. I was all alone with six girls. All of them came in skirts, and none of them was wearing underwear. They knew it was turning me on. Patricia, Susan, Nancy, Martha, Janet and Alice were names of the girls. Patricia stripped off my pants as she was jerking off my penis. Nancy was sucking it and Janet was already undressed.

I had my right hand on Janet's boobs as I fingered Alice. Since both Janet and Alice were standing, Susan climbed on their shoulders so as to have her pussy just in a line with my head.

I was licking it and I've never felt more pleasure doing so much of it at the same time. I stopped touching Janet's boobs and I stopped fingering Alice. Since both of them were free, Janet took Susan's left leg, and Alice took her right leg as they both raised her.

Susan was in a line with my dick and I was screwing her as she was hanging in the air holding her hands-on Janet's and Alice's shoulder. Susan got down on the floor.

Janet and Alice raised Martha in the air. There was something special about Martha, she was really on fire.

After that, those six girls climbed on the couch and turned their backs to me, I was licking the most intimate parts of their bodies.

When I started putting it inside of them, they were still in the same position. I screwed each of them and there was enough of sperm for everyone. It was something that they will never forget.

It's cold away from his bed
Chapter-10

I did some research later and I found out that the man that offered me to be my trainer was a very famous man. I called him and I told him that I would love to have him as a trainer. I was working very hard. I took a free day. I needed to rest myself. I needed to go for a walk and get some fresh air.

It was winter and everything was white and beautiful. Dead inside three years already, unable to get emotionally hurt, I felt nothing.

While everyone had a winter romance such as skating on the snow or kissing while snowflakes are falling on the ground, I was just having my hands in my pockets as I was walking the streets.

"Would you dare to walk over the river?"

"No way."

"But it's frozen, you're not going to fall through."

"How do you know what is the thickness of the snow?"

"I don't know, but last 10 days were extremely cold. I presume it's thick."

I was on a bridge, listening to the conversation of two girls. One of them had an incredibly similar voice to Marie.

I began to think about her. It's not that I felt much, but I was just remembering the time when I was so vulnerable, and yet so happy. I remembered the day when we hid from the rain. I remembered our first kiss. Leaned with my hands on the fence of the bridge, I was looking at the frozen river.

By the river, there was a sidewalk. These two girls were on the sidewalk, but still invisible, because they were just under the bridge.

Three years passed since I didn't see her, and in a few moments, she appeared by the river. I felt like something exploded in me.

Every memory that I reminded myself of those few minutes before I saw her, went again through my head. This time every memory was accompanied with an emotion of a high intensity. She and her female friend climbed up on the road and they headed to the bridge.

I don't know if she saw me, but I think that if she did, she would've definitely changed the direction of her walk.

I continued looking at the river as she was approaching the bridge. It was hard to recognize me since I had a cap on my head, I changed the way I dressed. I wasn't wearing loose clothes anymore, now it was more of a slim fit.

I was also much more muscled than I was when she saw me for the last time. She was walking the bridge and she passed by me.

"Marie."

She seemed like someone cut off her legs, she was standing on the bridge just like that, without any movement.

"Diane, can you leave me with this guy alone, please? We'll meet tomorrow again."

"Are you sure that it's smart for you to stay with him? Do you know him?"

"Yes, I know him. Don't worry."

"All right. See you then."

I was just looking at her as she started smiling. I was glad that she smiled, but I just couldn't. It was kinda fucked up for me to smile because I didn't smile for a long time.

"You changed." Said she.

"Oh well, a lot of time passed. You've changed as well."

"How are you?"

"I'm good. How are you?"

We were chatting. I was talking about my goals and about where I've been for the past three years. She didn't talk much, but she was curious and she asked a lot of questions.

"What about a cup of coffee?" I asked.

"Okay." Sad she.

We went to some place where she used to hang out. We were in a different city from the one where we used to be during the high school time.

After a nice talk about funny things that we went through during the high school period, she was looking at a cup of the coffee and tapping with her fingers. Her face was serious.

"Why did you do that to me? Why did you need another girl?"

"I tried to explain but you didn't want to hear the explanation."

"Why don't you just admit it?"

"Admit what? There was nobody but you in my heart! The girl that was embracing me that day in the GYM was a girl that I met a long time ago. That was a girl that I met before we a couple."

"Then why was she caressing your body that day when we were still a couple?"

"She came to me just like that and asked me if I forgot what was it like to be with her. She tried to seduce me once again. I said that I have a girlfriend and that I don't want to destroy my relationship with you, but she didn't listen to me. You have to believe me."

"Do you know how many nights I've spent crying? Do you know how many tears I shed? Millions of them."

"Look, I know that you felt bad inside, but you have to believe me. There was no girl but you in my heart,"

After a few minutes of silence, conversations continue.

"Neither did I feel good. When I heard that you have leukemia I was shocked. They said that you have very low chances to survive, and I couldn't imagine my sweetheart not walking under the same sky that I walk."

"That's true. Unfortunately, I had leukemia. Doctors estimated my chances are low, but you know me, I am a soldier. I underwent a bone marrow transplantation. Things are getting better now. Look, no matter how much you hurt me, I was still there in the crowd when you won the rap battle. When you said that you love me in front of all of those people, I think that I was the only one that cried that night.

I sat down next to her and I kissed her. She looked at my eyes and she just hit me with that smile. Every time I see her smiling, it's like someone is giving me a heart massage, full of emotions.

She hugged me firmly and said: "I don't want to separate myself from you anymore. Winter isn't white, the sky isn't blue and heart isn't red without you. Only the autumn was the same. At that time drops of the rain were falling along with leaves, and I fell apart.

Naked, and showing his masculinity
Chapter-11

We went to a place where she lived. While I was coming through the hall of her house and as I entered her room I remembered those motivational quotes that were hanging on the wall of the GYM. I realized that getting Marie back into my life was a success as well, and for the first time in my life, I considered love as a success.

It was really hard to connect with her once again, and I managed to do that. Once again I was alive being, with feelings. Once we were on the bed, It wasn't just a sexual desire. I wanted to feel her as a person, as someone that I loved. I didn't just want to feel her body.

I was kissing her hair as roses in the vase were kissing the air. Our pulses were throbbing in the same rhythm. The fire in a fireplace was dancing with the same intensity of lust in every little sparkle.

My hands were spontaneously stripping off every part of clothes she had on her body. We were both in the fire of our needs and only body-to-body relation could serve as a water to satisfy the needs.

Gentle movements of our connected bodies made the bed shake.

We always had that problem that my penis was too big for her, but she said that it's okay and that I should go gentle on her making sure that she ends up with orgasm. "Oh yeah, that's what you need to do to me". She shouted.

We stood up, and I put her hands above the fireplace, I spread her legs as I was putting it inside. Her vagina was so close to the fire that it burned her hair down there. Our genitals were so hot. When I finished I ejaculated inside the fire as she embraced my neck with one hand, and squeezed all the sperm from my penis with another hand.

"Your breath is so warm."

"I can drive you to whatever temperatures you want!" I answered.

At the end we were both sighing, that was a pleasure searching for a sound.

"I love you." She said.

"I love you too." I replied.

After that, I left her house.

The sexy guy posing by the moon
Chapter-12

Months were passing and our love grew bigger than it was when we were in the high school. I had, even more, motivation to work my way to becoming a model.

I had a great trainer. Everything was going perfectly except one thing – Marie was sick once again.

One day, while I was walking the street, it was very windy. Some kind of windy circle appeared out of nowhere and caught me. The same moment I was at some strange and dark place. The only light that could be perceived there was a light of some planets.

Between two planets, one black and one white, I've seen a man from the fast food, who said that I have potential. He was having a rap battle against my professor of physics, the one from high school.

They were fighting and professor of physics won. Professor of physics approached me, he had a strange scar on his forehead.

A scar looked like a thunder. He approached me, raised his eyebrow with his forefinger and said:

Did you really think that he can win? This is my territory; I know everything about moving in time and space. Rapping is all about speed, about moving your hands and tongue as fast as possible. I never liked you and I don't want to take a risk of you succeeding in your life.

You won the rap battle back then in the high school although I claimed that you are worthless. I'm not going to let you become a model because accomplishment of your dream is for me a nightmare. Get ready to die. He pulled out a gun and aimed at my head.

At the moment when he wanted to pull the trigger, a white planet started shining incredibly, it shined so much that I couldn't move. When the shine lowered, I opened my eyes and I've seen that planet was pulling professor of physics to the surface. Professor was stuck at the surface of the planet as planet exploded along with the professor. Few moments after that, I heard a voice:

"Don't let him see it."

As soon as I heard that, I was back on the street again.

A man that led me to 7th sky
Chapter-13

It was a big day for me. I came to her apartment. She was lying in a bed. She said that she doesn't feel good. She said that she was sick again.

I've never seen her face more beautiful than that day. I was lying next to her and even though she was weak, she still wanted me to make her love. I was kissing her and coming down her body with my fingers. Her body was wet and she was on fire more than she had ever been.

It was obvious that she tried her best to give me as much pleasure as she could. She was lying in a straight position and I was lying upside down. We had an oral sex for forty minutes.

It was an incredible pleasure for both of us. With our bodies wet, I started putting my penis inside her. She was screaming more than ever.

"You're the only cure that I have." Said she.

I was going gentle on her but she was going hard on me, she was jumping on my penis with her vagina with a big pressure. She bent over the bad as I was putting it from behind.

An hour passed since our sex started. I spread her legs as much as possible, as she was keeping her balance holding her hands on the table. Silence covered her house as she was lying in my lap so tired that she couldn't say a word.

That was the day that I walked the stage for the first time. I officially became a model. I was happy more than ever, but that feeling didn't last long. Few days after I became a model, she died.

I write under the pseudonym: Urquhart Randolph. I like to write great romance stories that take you on a blazing journey - tears, laughter (may be both) or just a steamy hot fun (perhaps all of them).

Please... leave a review, regardless if you think my book deserves 1* or 5 * let me know if you had enjoyed this great story?

THANK YOU ☺

VISIT US
WWW.GLOFTON.COM
Enroll in our VIP list.
Be the first to be notified on our latest published book.
Downloading for free gifts.